The
Lonely
Peach

The Lonely Peach

Daniel Eisan

Copyright © 2011 by Daniel Eisan.

ISBN: Softcover   978-1-4628-5634-3

ISBN: Softcover   978-1-4628-5634-3
             Ebook   978-1-4628-5635-0

This is a work of fiction. Names, characters, places and incidents either are the product of the author's imagination or are used fictitiously, and any resemblance to any actual persons, living or dead, events, or locales is entirely coincidental.

This book was printed in the United States of America.

To order additional copies of this book, contact:
Xlibris Corporation
0-800-644-6988
www.xlibrispublishing.co.uk
Orders@xlibrispublishing.co.uk
301855

-ACKNOWLEDGEMENTS-

I would like to express my thanks to those who
have helped me during the production
of this book.
In particular:

Sharon Pease

Pat Finn

Sandra Gilliott

Kieren Hudson (Illustrations)

Once upon a time, in a field not so far away, there was a peach tree. It was a beautiful tree; it stood on its own, surrounded by daisies and dandelions and had a view that went on for miles.

Then one day a man named farmer Green walked up to the tree and said, "my, my, I'm going to sell a lot of peaches this year." He started to pick the peaches off the tree one by one and put them into his little basket, and then when his basket was full to the top, he walked off to his van and drove off back to his farm.

Farmer Green unloaded his basket, put the peaches in a bowl and washed them in the sink; he then walked out of the room. All of a sudden the peaches came to life, one by one, out popped a left arm, a right arm, a left leg, and right leg, two eyes, a nose and a mouth, they all looked the same but one was a little different, this peach, Percy had a keen sense for adventure, he knew he was going to be sold on the market, so instead of staying with the other peaches he jumped off the counter, onto the floor and hid behind the table leg.

Farmer Green entered the room again and started to count the peaches, he thought he had all forty-nine but as he turned around he saw a peach on the floor, that peach, was Percy. Farmer Green walked over, knelt over and picked up Percy, washed him again and placed him with the other peaches, Percy had a very angry look on his face, but he bottled it up and went to sleep.

Next morning Percy was woken by the screaming noise of a cockerel, he looked around, rubbed his eyes, and said to himself "This is the day, I will escape", farmer Green walked into the kitchen, and said "Morning my little peaches, today you're going to make me quite a bit of money", he picked up the peaches and put them into a brown paper bag, Percy managed to hide behind the kettle barely slipping away from the firm grasp of Farmer Greens rather filthy hand.

Percy stayed hidden until he heard the loud bang of the old wooden door closing behind Farmer Green's back, Percy, slowly but surely peeped his head around the side of the kettle, looked around, and sighed with relief.

Percy jumped off the counter and headed towards a crack in the door, he just managed to squeeze through, Percy looked around, took a deep breath of fresh air and began his journey of travelling, "Here I go" Percy said to himself, he began to take his first few steps to freedom, being so full of excitement.

Unfortunately Percy was not paying attention to the oncoming traffic, he suddenly heard the honk of a speeding lorry, Percy's face dropped, his eyes widened and his mouth gaped, he jumped across to the other side of the road, just missing the wheels, the lorry continued on down the road as Percy sat on the grass trying to catch his breath.

Percy got back up, wiped himself down, and continued walking; about fifteen minutes later he approached a little village. He walked along the narrow cobble streets, until he saw a little fruit shop, he could smell the strawberries and apples, he slowly approached it, but then suddenly he saw Farmer Green handing a bag of fruit over to an old lady. Percy quickly hid behind a box of grapes, he peeped his head round the corner, he saw that Farmer Green had gone back inside the shop.

Percy wiped his brow and said "Phew, that was close; I can't imagine what would have happened if I was caught by Farmer Green I could have been sold off to that lady".

Percy started to continue along the cobbled street, he looked up towards the sky, as he did this the wind started to pick up, clouds turned grey and started to gather together, then in one almighty boom, there was a crack of thunder.

Percy had never seen anything like this before, he started to panic, he ran away to find shelter, the rain started to fall all around him, big splashes of water fell on Percy's head, he fell down into a big muddy puddle. He got up, didn't bother to wipe himself down, he just kept on going, Percy quickly turned to go round a corner but a big brown dog started to bark at him and tried to climb a fence to get to Percy.

Percy screamed, quickly turned around and ran towards a place for shelter, five minutes later he came to an old abandoned shed in the middle of a field. Percy walked inside; pigeons that had already made a home there flew about the roof as Percy walked about.

Percy found a big pile of hay, he climbed on top, put some over the top of himself and used it for a bed, Percy started to close his eyes, he thought to himself, "It's okay Percy, this is only the first day" then before he could say goodnight, he fell asleep.

The sun began to rise over grassy hills, all around; you could see the sun shining off the morning dew on the fresh cut grass. An old cockerel jumped onto the old wooden fence, and it forced its chest forward and with one deep breath it made the morning cry "Cock-a-doodle-doo!" Percy jumped up in shock, he looked around to see what the noise was, he realized that it was outside.

Percy moved the hay away from his body, rubbed his eyes and climbed down from the pile and landed softly on the ground.

He went outside, said bye to the old little shack and continued to go on his journey, Percy walked along the side of the road, and it was all going fine. Percy was happy and whistling to himself when all of a sudden from out of the big apple tree, a big black crow came swooping down, it grasped Percy within its big claw like feet, "Help, Help!" Percy shouted, but he was too high for anyone to be able to hear him.

The crow dropped Percy in its big nest made of sticks and mud, Percy thought he was safe until he turned around to see three hatched eggs with three slightly bald squealing baby crows, Percy screamed, he decided to sit near the edge of the nest in hope that he would be able to climb to safety.

The mother crow flew away from the nest to get worms for the babies,

Percy sat perfectly still, and he started to look around for a quick exit, then suddenly he saw that the nest was in between two branches. Both leading to the centre of the tree, Percy gently stood up and quietly moved around the edge of the nest where one of the branches were, Percy climbed out and balanced on the branch.

He started to walk around the branch looking towards him at all time, trying to not look down, Percy looked to the side of him and in the distance saw the mother crow soaring back to her nest, she looked at Percy, squawked and began to speed up towards him, for a moment time seemed to stand still.

Percy couldn't move, then from out of nowhere a sudden boost of courage and energy came over Percy, he began to run across the branch and before he knew it, he was on the other side; he took cover behind a few leaves whilst the mother crow fed her young.

Percy took some time to get his breath back "That was close" he said to himself, but it wasn't over, the mother crow raised her head and looked towards where Percy had ran to, Percy's eyes widened in horror, he didn't have or want time to think, he just got up and looked for a quick way out,

The mother crow hopped onto the branch and began to hop towards Percy, and still Percy struggled to escape, just the thought of having those tight clutches around his body again made Percy sick to his stomach, then for some strange reason, he looked down and saw a hole that seemed to lead to the very bottom of the tree.

The Mother crow was getting much closer to Percy at this point, then all of a sudden she flew straight towards Percy at a great speed, without thinking Percy closed his eyes and jumped down the hole.

On his way down Percy could feel the air whooshing past his face, "Woo" he shouted as he sped down the bark of the tree, then all of a sudden the tree seemed to curve and Percy shot off up into the air and landed on a soft patch of grass about a meter away from the tree.

Percy looked up to see the mother crow circling the tree and squawking very loudly looking for Percy, Percy wiped his forehead "It seems this whole outdoors real life thing can be hard".

Percy continued his journey and before he knew it, it was night time again, and because he had left the little old shack he had nowhere indoors to sleep, so instead he found a hole that had been burrowed in a nearby hill, Percy knew that it wouldn't be comfortable but still he spent the night.

The next morning Percy was awoke by the beautiful colours of the sunrise shining in his eyes, his eyes opened, closed then opened fully, Percy rubbed his eyes and stretched his arms way out into the air, so that he was fully awake, Percy climbed out of the little hole that he called home for the night, and once again started to walk off to somewhere else.

Percy suddenly found himself on an old dusty road, it seemed to stretch for miles and miles, Percy didn't think that he could last a journey as long as that,

but, being the brave strong peach that he was, he

took a few deep breaths and started to walk along

the road.

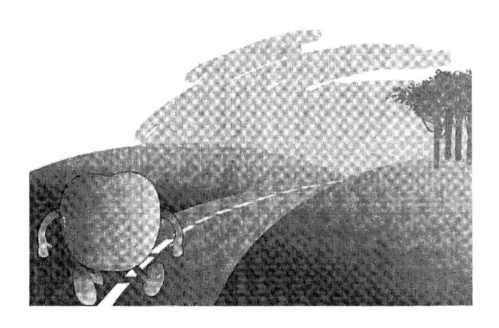

Percy was now in a world of his own walking along the middle of the road, he did not hear the cars driving past him, then suddenly Percy heard a loud honking noise, he looked up to see a great big lorry speeding towards him, Percy remembered the lorry from the first time he nearly got run over.

Percy started to run to the side of the road, but all of a sudden, Percy once again found himself in the clutches of another big bird.

Percy's eyes were tightly closed; he thought that he daren't open them, then the next thing he knew he was lightly placed on the branch of a big old oak tree, Percy opened his eyes, and he looked around to see acres of woodland filled with trees of all different sizes.

Percy looked beside him to see an old grey mother owl, "Hello there" said the owl, for a moment Percy was silent, "I'm not going to hurt you" the mother continued. "Who . . . who are you?" asked Percy in a nervous voice; "I'm Olivia, Olivia the Owl" replied the Owl.

"Hi, Olivia, my name is Percy, I'm all alone, I ran away because Farmer Green was going to sell me in the market, he took all my brothers and sisters away but I managed the escape."

"Oh my" said Olivia, "That sounds dangerous" she continued, "It is, I've nearly been hurt so many times over the past few days, I was captured by a crow and everything." Olivia began to tut," "Well

I'm glad the mean old crow didn't hurt you little one, but you're safe now".

"Will you be my friend Olivia?" asked Percy hopefully, Olivia giggled, and replied "Of course I will." Percy smiled to himself.

Then all of a sudden a tear trickled down Percy's cheek, Olivia took Percy under her wing and hugged him, "What's wrong Percy?" asked Olivia, "What should I do Olivia, I've lost all my family and I can't go back to Farmer Green but I can't stay out in the wild, it's too dangerous." "Well Percy maybe that's something you should have thought about before you ran away, you know maybe we can save some of your family, if we fly quickly enough", Percy's face lit up "Really Olivia!".

"Hop on my back, and hold on tight," Percy did as Olivia said, and off they went flying to the local Farmer's market, when they reached the market place, Percy and Olivia started to search for Farmer

Green, but it was very hard because there were lots of people all huddled up together, Percy began to think that it was impossible to find Farmer Green until he heard "five peaches for a pound!"

"That's Farmer Green's voice!" Percy shouted. Olivia swooped down above Farmer Green's head as he was just about to hand over a bag of peaches to an old man, the bag fell back into the box, Olivia landed on the box, Farmer Green was very angry, then he saw Percy on Olivia's back, "Is that you Percy? The one that got away," "yes, and I'm very mad at you!, you took away my brothers and sisters away to sell them!"

Farmer Green's face went from angry to concerned, he then smiled, well Percy, it would seem that this year hasn't been good and I haven't sold many, in fact I've sold non from the tree I picked you from." "But, I saw you sell a lot of peaches to an elderly woman two days ago" replied Percy. Farmer Green chuckled, "Oh my Percy, they were other farmer's peaches, he asked me to sell his load whilst we went out to pick his daughter Lucy up from school."

Percy's face lit up once more, "So all my brothers and sisters are still here?" "Yes they are Percy." replied Farmer Green happily. Farmer Green picked up three see through bags from a box and inside were all of Percy's brothers and sisters.

"PERCY!" they all shouted with joy, Farmer Green opened all three bags, and all of the peaches ran towards Percy and Percy ran towards them, they all came together in one giant hug; they all started giggling and smiling.

Percy looked over towards Olivia, she smiled, "Wait there guys." Percy ran over to Olivia and hugged her tightly, "Please come live with us Olivia." Olivia looked down at Percy, "I would love to but it's up to Farmer Green." replied Olivia, "Wait here." said Percy excitedly.

Percy ran up to Farmer Green, Farmer Green looked down at Percy and knelt down so they could see each other properly, "Farmer Green?" Percy said shyly, "Yes Percy?" Percy cleared his throat and said "Would it be ok if my new friend Olivia the Owl came to live with us?" for a moment there was no reply, Farmer Green rubbed his Black beard, looked at Olivia, then back at Percy then said "Of course she can, I would love to have a barn owl".

Percy jumped with joy, and ran over to Olivia, "Olivia, Olivia, farmer Green said yes", Olivia hooted and flew over to Farmer Green and landed on his shoulder.

"Thank you Farmer Green, for letting me come live on your farm", "You're very welcome Olivia", "Come on everybody back into the van, let's go home."

They all got in the van started to drive down the dusty road, before they knew it they were home, Farmer Green walked into the living room and put on the fire; he made everyone a cup of hot cocoa.

"Come on Percy tell us about your adventure." said one of Percy's sisters with great excitement, Percy smiled took a quick drink of his cocoa and began to speak, "Hmm where should I begin?" Percy began to tell everyone how he escaped from the house and all the troubles he got himself into and about the mother crow. But as it was getting late everyone was starting to yawn, and before Percy could finish his story, one by one they all fell asleep by the nice warm fire.

THE END

Lightning Source UK Ltd.
Milton Keynes UK
177423UK00001B/129/P